I0615343

John W. Montclair

Real and Ideal

John W. Montclair

Real and Ideal

ISBN/EAN: 9783337049775

Printed in Europe, USA, Canada, Australia, Japan

Cover: Foto ©Andreas Hilbeck / pixelio.de

More available books at **www.hansebooks.com**

Real and Ideal.

J. W. MONTCLAIR.

REAL AND IDEAL

BY

JOHN W. MONTCLAIR,

PHILADELPHIA:

FREDERICK LEYPOLDT.

NEW-YORK:
HURD & HOUGHTON.
F. W. CHRISTERN.

BOSTON:
A. K. LORING,
S. R. URBINO.

LONDON:
TRÜBNER & COMPANY,

1865.

FRANCIS HART & CO., PRINTERS AND STATIONERS,
63 CORTLANDT STREET, NEW-YORK.

TO

HENRY W. LONGFELLOW:

AN

HUMBLE TRIBUTE IN ADMIRATION OF HIS TASTE,
LEARNING, AND GENIUS.

" Unheralded — a pilgrim and a stranger;

If ye would know me, keep me company."

REAL AND IDEAL.

PROLOGUE.

"Dread son of Saturn, what word hast thou spoken?"— HOMER.
"To be or not to be—that is the question."— SHAKSPEARE.
"— In judgment nothing, if not critical."— QUARTERLY REVIEW

YE kingly umpires, when ye condescend
To scan the lines that court your chary praise,
Search not alone the rhymster's awkward turns,
And frame them out, to draw the vulgar gaze :

But seek, with fertilizing sympathy
And warmth, the germs of promise to unfold ;
Much that at first seems dross-like in the ore,
May be refined to bars of mental gold.

The poet's weal is oftenest in your keep—
For minstrel ne'er full-grown to life has sprung ;
E'en Shakspeare wandered on uneven paths,
And Chaucer lisped in numbers ere he sung.

2

Ere Wordsworth and Lord Byron reached a goal,
Feeble the sound that first conveyed their name;
'Till willing ears were strengthened to their harps:
Then the wide welkin echoed of their fame.

Clearer to think what others thought before—
Keenly to feel th' afflictions of our race—
Better to say what others oft have said—
Such merits win the Minnesinger's place.

Not phrenzied in somnambulistic trance,
Nor, Sibyl-like, in mysticism lost,
Would we attest to logic's steadfast friends
That lack of sense must be the poet's cost.

But we would strive, like sonneteer Petrarch,
Suggestive and condensed our aims to tell;
That o'er an out-line page the reader's mind
In self-thought volumes lingering may dwell.

Nor would we forge frail copies of ourselves,
Like gifted minds, when, restive, they have sought
To swing the hammer of heroic youth
Upon the anvil of their rusted thought

The chosen bards, who sang for three-score years—
Our laureled three, grown old and bearded gray—
Who hummed the cradle songs of stalwart men—
Slowly, like swans, must sing their lives away.

Through fifty solar orbits one of these
Copied the woods and fields, mountains and sky:
Flawless reflected by his argent mind
These pictures, photographed, before us lie.

A second learnt the Chronicles-of-Eld,
To open treasures many long had sought:
Bright burns the flame of his magician-lamp,
To light the shores that bound the sea of thought.

The other's lyre told of Athenian lands—
Of hearts that bled by suffering and wrong;
His wit is love, his grief is hope deferred:
Their keenness glistens in his saddest song.

When these retire, shall harmony be mute—
Must native voice of melody be sealed?
Strike, younger bards, your chords on newer harps,
That newer promises may be revealed!

There yet remain proud themes for other strains:
To draw the picture of these later days—
To cull the flowers that grow in distant fields,
And plant the foreign seed on native ways;

To draw the lines of cis-Atlantic scenes—
To sing the legends of Powhatan's times—
To chant the hymn of "Paradise Preserved"—
To ring the bells of Freedom in our rhymes!

FLOWERS.

BE welcomed evermore, ye lovely sprites!
My greeting lips in homage touch your robes.
From out the debris of departed things,
By some strange magic starting from the ground,
Ye breathe, and live a silent, sainted life:
The while ye nod and flutter in the air,
Your fragrance rises, like a welcomed prayer;
Your colors blend, akin to sunset hues;
Your forms are shapes that fairies well might choose.
Would ye could tarry here: in this rude world
Too soon ye droop; by human touch profaned,
Ye shrink, and slowly wither at my side.
Whence came ye—tell me, whither do ye hide?
Do unseen spirits weave your gossamer shroud?
Do ye dissolve, to rise a silvery cloud?
Would that this clay, beyond life's measured hours,
In ashes laid might change to lovely flowers;
That o'er some silent and forsaken tomb
Again in living emblems I might bloom.

THE PILGRIMAGE TO KEVLAAR.

TRANSLATED FROM THE GERMAN OF HEINE.

I.

THE mother stood at the window,
On the bed her sick son lay;
"Arise and come hither, dear William,
The procession is coming this way."

"I am very feeble, dear mother,
Too faint to listen or see;
When I think of dying Gretchen,
The world seems all lost to me."

"Come forth with rosary and prayer-book,
Let us both for Kevlaar depart;
'Tis there that the mother of Jesus
Heals many an aching heart."

From spires gay flags were flying,
In the streets solemn chants were sung ;
And as the procession moved onward,
All the bells of Cologne were rung.

Soon the throng was joined by two pilgrims—
A mother, with son by her side ;
And both sang " Ora pro nobis "
To Mary, the heavenly bride.

II.

The mother of Jesus at Kevlaar
To-day wears her costliest gown ;
For they say that she will be busy
With the many cripples in town.

The lame and sick crowd around her,
With the numerous offerings they bring :
Waxen arms, waxen legs do they offer—
Waxen hearts—waxen many a thing.

For to him that offers a wax hand,
The wound on his own hand shall heal ;
And he that offers a wax leg,
No longer leg pains shall feel.

To Kevlaar went many on crutches
Who now can dance on the rope;
And some now play the viola,
That were palsied in hand beyond hope.

The mother she took a wax taper,
And moulded it into a heart:
" Son, offer this to the Blessed Virgin,
That your anguish, for aye, may depart."

Soon did he kneel with his offering
To the image so holy and blest;
As teardrops rolled from his eyelids,
Agony streamed from his breast.

" Thou saintly mother of Jesus,
Thou spotless and heavenly queen,
My poor heart from sin and suffering,
Thy mercy alone can clean.

" My mother and self are dwelling
In proud Cologne, on the Rhine;
'Tis a city of stately churches,
Whose many altars are thine.

" Adjoining our cottage lived Gretchen ;—
She is dead now, and laid to rest.
This waxen heart do I bring thee—
Wilt thou heal the wound in my breast ?

" Mend thou my heart's deep anguish,
And morning and night, each day,
Through life will I chant thy glory,
And many a litany pray."

III.

When the suffering youth and his mother
Had returned to their chamber small,
There at night time the Blessed Virgin
Entered unknown to all.

She bent o'er the feeble one gently,
And laying her hand so light
On the beating heart of the sleeper,
She smiled—and vanished from sight.

In a dream the mother beheld it,
Like a vision that moved in a cloud ;
And as she awoke from her slumber
The dogs were barking aloud.

Her son lay stretched beside her,
Quiet, and cold, and dead;
And his sunken cheek was gleaming
Like a rose, in the morning's red.

The mother her hands she folded,
Faintly she sank on her knee;
And the only words she could utter
Were " Ave, Ave Marie."

BELLS BY NIGHT.

'Tis Sabbath eve: from the old kirk tower
Merrily chime the bells by night;
The organ peals with thrilling power,
And the windows glow with holy light—
Merrily chime the bells by night.

Year by year to the pilgrim throng
Warningly speak the bells by night:
" Life is short, eternity's long;
Children of darkness waken to light"—
Warningly say the bells by night.

Over the grave of the patriot slain
Solemnly rolls a dirge by night:
" The good are gathered, like ripened grain—
Why should we weep when angels delight ?"
Solemnly echo the bells by night.

3

Lone do I list to a curfew bell
That woefully throbs within me to-night!
Of waning life its pulsations tell;
And many a legend does memory recite,
That *mournfully* wrings my heart to-night!

ODE TO POESY.

ERE Memnon's shadow
Touched charmed ground—
When time, an infant,
Scarce winged his flight—
Through the long night
Of countless ages,
Ever the minstrel's
Echoes resound.

Bard, be thou welcome,
Who canst inspire
Like seer or prophet,
And wake the lyre
Of thousand strings!

Thy strains melodious
Earth's future millions
Are yet to sing.
Thou fill'st the goblet
With draught refreshing,
For wearied pilgrims,
That thirst to quaff
Ethereal streams.

In the lone forest
To thee the warbling
Of bird is worship,
And wild-wood rustlings
Are spoken language.
Thou picturest beauty
In desolation.
The crowded highway,
Where wealth, usurping,
Loads man with labor,
To thee is only
A tomb of silence.
Thy words are blessings,
And quick relief;
For the heart-stricken,
Thou softenest grief;

To youthful pleasures
Givest virtues tone —
Yea, music's measures
Are all thine own !
The hearts of heroes
By thee are nerved ;
The lips of beauty
By thee are moved ;
Woman's devotion
Oft thou hast proved :
No better knight
Her cause has served.

On the far ocean,
Upon the mountain
And on the plain,
From fields of battle,
Breathed as in prayer
Like saintly word,
Thy voice is heard.
In holy temples
Thy strains are sung ;
Thy words from breaking
Hearts are wrung.

Thus, self-ennobled,
By thine own genius,
Fame's torch is fired:
By sages quoted,
In learned orations,
Thy texts are noted;
And shine through ages
On deathless pages!

THE HAUNTED LAKE.

SUBJECT FROM THE GERMAN.

The story of the "Naiad" is an old and favorite one in German minstrelsy. Goethe (in the "Fisher"), Heine (in the "Loreley"), and recent authors of less note, present greatly differing versions of the same interesting poetic subject.

HIGH on the cedar mountain
  Nestles a deep blue lake,
And lilies float upon it,
  White as a snowy flake.

A shepherd youth went thither,
  Estray from flock and kine;
He saw the beauteous flowers:
  " Sweet things, ye must be mine."

As he his crook extended
  To reach the lovely prize,
Behold from 'neath the waters
  A maiden's hand arise.

It seized a flower and drew it
　　Beneath the watery deep:
" Come, follow where my secret
　　Together we may keep.

" Away from idle searches,
　　These lilies root beneath;
Reach me thy hand, I'll lead thee
　　To twine my bridal wreath."

The shepherd did not follow:
　　In loneness, he repined—
For never could he banish
　　The pale flower from his mind.

He wandered on the mountain,
　　He seemed to fade away;
Nor have the woodmen met him
　　Since that eventful day.

THE SPIRIT'S REVELATION

FORMS beloved, whose memory haunts me,
In mementoes near me dwell;
Oft they come in evening visions,
Or in dreams their legends tell.

Sad and lonely, but unspoken
Fancy reaches far away—
When some sudden thrill awakes me,
And a seraph seems to say:

" Though we may not break the secret
That the gates of death reveal,
In the grey night's gloom and stillness
Drawn toward the earth we feel.

" For there is a strange communion
'Twixt men and our spirit band;
Oft in omens we approach ye,
Brethren of our ancient land.

" From the glittering orb of even,
Gliding down upon its beams,
Noiseless as the step of Zephyr,
Do we visit you in dreams.

" At the couch of all true-hearted
Stand we guardian, in their sleep;
For the loved ones left behind us
Do we faithful vigils keep.

" See, yon spirit mother hovers
O'er her fondly cherished child—
Weeps in smiles of tender sorrow—
Drinks its breath, with rapture wild.

" Playing with her flowing tresses,
Pillowed on her heaving breast,
Comes the spirit child, to linger,
By its mother's lips caressed.

" And the ghostly husband beckons
To his mourning, faithful wife ;
In yon lunar dwelling bids her
Join with him in spirit life."

Never can the tic be severed
'Twixt the hearts that truly love ;
And for every friend departed
One ye gain in heaven above.

THE GAME OF CHESS.

CALMLY as an enchanter, oft beside the checkered field,
I sit, to guide the puppets small, that mimic history yield.
Quick, as the sun of thought sends action to their pulse-
    less bone,
Each little form is made to fill a purpose not its own.

Move on, ye ranks of soldier-pawns, deep mingle in the
    fight —
No refuge shall this castle yield unto the errant knight —
Yon mitred bishop low shall bend, when king and queen
    have fled,
And soon this hand, omnipotent, shall lay them with the
    dead!

This is my Coliseum, where in gladiatorial strife,
Perdition-doomed be every one to whom I gave a life;
I register no slavish skill, I heed not chess-born woe:
None on that board shall e'er aspire my purposes to know!

Thus men, 'neath banners black and white, with longings
    all innate,
Like puppets, follow out their course, led by the hand
    of fate;
And each brief trial tells this tale: that nought is left to
    choose
Where e'en the bravest comes to grief, and winners too
    must lose.

Tis passion leads us all astray, wrapt in delusive thought;
Vain in this labyrinthine world enduring hold is sought;
The spring that moves our heart is wound its numbered
    ticks to last;
Life's fleeting record only shews the agony of the past.

THE OLD COMEDIAN.

TRANSLATED FROM THE GERMAN OF A. GRÜN.

THE footlights blaze, the curtains rise,
And peering are a thousand eyes
Where tinselled jugglers strut apace;
With paint begrimed each truthless face.

You mountebank of snowy hair,
I well could draw his home despair;
Poor, worn-out, crippled harlequin,
His efforts fail respect to win.

Whilst honored age, though lorn and weak,
A tutorage with youth may seek,
This old, obedient, hired clown
Racks his stiff joints to please the town.

Old men, they court repose by night ;
The aged arm forgets its might ;
'Tis raised to guide, or to caress—
'Tis folded prayerful, and to bless.

Those trembling hands hang by his side ;
Those valiant lips his limbs deride ;
And when to points the text may soar,
With loud guffaw the groundlings roar.

Though chronic pains may pinch his frame,
He must be Momus, ever the same ;
To those who see him night by night,
His tears would prove a rare delight.

But lo ! how faint the actor speaks :
He falters, and an exit seeks.
" Old Thespian, hast forgot thy cue ?
Thy walk's unsteady, thy text untrue ! "

In vain the old comedian tries
To silence insult ; murmurs rise ;
Away he totters with alarm,
And falls within the prompter's arm.

On comedy the curtains rose;
On tragedy the players close.
The vulgar crowd, they whistle and cry
A dying actor's litany.

Behind the curtains, within a chair,
Ruddy of cheek and brown of hair,
A corpse is resting; its brow is cold,
And on it a painted lie is told.

For the mien that made the idle laugh,
It looks a solemn epitaph;
False and hollow is all we see—
His life, his art, were mockery!

Never will rustle in nature's breeze
Those faded, painted, canvass trees;
And the oily moon that gleams o'erhead
Never learned to weep for the dead.

From a motley group, 'neath a tattered sky,
Comes one to speak this eulogy:
" He fought and fell, as heroes yield,
Upon the *drama's* battle-field."

Then a dancing girl, as a beggarly muse,
Upon his brow, with shabby excuse,
Pressed a laurel wreath that some Cæsar had worn —
A paper invention. dirty and torn.

His funeral procession numbered two ;
Brief was the pageant, the costs were few ;
And as they laid him away to rest,
I heard no pity, I heard no jest.

RAMBLER AND SHEPHERD.

" HAPPY Shepherd,
 Piping thy lay,
 Where the flocks
 Are dancing at play;
 Life-companion
 Of lambs and flowers,
 Counting in roses
 The toilsome hours;

" Though thrush and linnet
 Have sung in vain,
 Thy artless ditties
 My heart regain;
 And world's ambition
 Is all forgot
 In leafy dwelling
 And shepherd lot!"

" Wanderer, to childhood,
   Gentle and meek,
I may in prattle
   Oft eloquent speak;
And for the maiden
   My strains can swell
To sweet responses
   No lips dare tell."

More would he say—
   But steps drew near:
Louder he pipes
   The melody clear;
Sweetly vibrating
   Resounds a lute,
Mingling concord
   With pastoral flute.

Nodding ringlets
   And eyes are seen,
That smile on the shepherd,
   From over the green;
Ah, their lustre—
   It told of more
Than all that the shepherd
   Had hinted before.

" Shepherd, thy pastimes
My dreams fulfil :
Lend me thy pipe,
And teach me thy skill ;
Yield me thy magic —
Train me thy ways —
That I too may share
In Arcadian days ! "

Then spake the maiden,
Archly, and wise :
" Fertile our valley,
And quiet our skies ;
But to be happy—"
She whispered to me—
" You, like shepherds,
In love must be."

VESUVIUS.

THY greeting, fairest Italy,
In numbers I would sing;
Thy waves, thy skies, thy women's eyes
Their sparkling offerings bring.

Thy lovely bay's cerulean waves
Refresh my famished eyes;
Earth's towering altar flames on high—
Olympian grandeurs rise.

I view a living pyramid—
A cauldron self-renewed—
A cousin of the lunar peaks—
A monster unsubdued.

Wave-bound, on far Sicilia's isle,
Thy brother, Ætna, sleeps,
Whom, like a captive Titan king,
Neptune in durance keeps.

Linked with a grander fate art thou;
Proud Naples kneels to thee,
Thoughtful of Herculaneum.
Beneath the molten sea.

'Twas when thy minions laid waste
This now sepulchral spot,
Where spectres of the past arise,
Of households long forgot.

From hollow voice came thy commands—
In wrath thy white beard shook;
Tempests arose and sunlight paled
'Neath thy defiant look.

Aloft in air the wild birds screamed,
The wild beasts moaned with fear;
From herded men the frantic cry
Replaced both prayer and tear.

They perished all, and chaos came
Like deluge passed away ;
Where villa, grot and temple stood
A pall of ashes lay.

Slain were thy guards, fair Pompeii—
Thy hosts, thy guests, have fled ;
Strangers now quaff from Cæsar's vaults,
And drink to—Cæsar's dead.

Old mount, though thou hast Sodom's fate
Transplanted to thy home,
Thou gains't for art rich legacy
From old, imperial Rome.

ERL KING'S DAUGHTER.

FROM AN OLD TEUTONIC LEGEND.

Longfellow's "Poets and Poetry of Europe," in a translation entitled "Sir Olof's Bridal,"
presents a Swedish version of this ancient ballad. It would seem that Goethe, when
composing his "Erl King," derived several hints from the materials of the present
poem. Professor Aytoun alludes to this circumstance, in a note appended to his translations of the "Poems and Ballads of Goethe," and also renders a version of the present
ballad

'TWAS night in the forest. Sir Oluf rode by;
He had summoned his wedding company.

Shadows were dancing on the green land;
The Erl King's daughter grasped his hand.

"Welcome, Sir Oluf; turn not to flee:
Join our revels, and dance with me.

"I may not dance, I must not stay,
For to-morrow will be my bridal day."

"Listen, Sir Oluf: come join with me,
And these spurs of gold thy trophies shall be.

" Wear this robe of gossamer slight,
   That I've woven, and bleached by the pale moon-light."

"My vow is another's, time calls away ;
   I must to the castle ere dawn of day."

" Relent, noble knight, and enter our ranks ;
   These jewels shall be my token of thanks."

" Thy gems are welcome, with them will I ride,
   To adorn at the altar my trusting bride."

He took from the elf maid a glittering flower :
Sir Oluf was hers from that very hour !

His heart was smitten with pangs so sore,
That he quailed as he never had done before.

Fainting, she lifted him on his steed :
The iron-cased warrior of help had need !

When his steed regained the castle gate,
Long had his mother been standing in wait.

" Whence comest thou, by dawn, my child ?
   Thy features are pallid, thy look is wild !"

5

"Mother, I'm faint, and unnerved by fright;
I met the Erl King's daughter this night!"

"Get thee to couch; evil haunts thee, son;
Thy vows are forfeit, thy bridal's undone!"

"Tell the fair lady that I may be found,
Training the falcon and coursing the hound."

Soon morning broke; by the sunlight clear,
Both bride and wedding guests appear.

They spread the feast, they poured the wine:
"Where is Sir Oluf, the bridegroom mine?

"Is the gallant knight riding at morn
In the tangled forest, estray and lorn?"

They search the wildwood for many an hour;
They scan the castle, from vault to tower.

By the shrieking bride the guests stand aghast:
In a lowly chamber they found him at last.

Sir Oluf—in death on his couch he lay:
The elf maid had stolen his life away.

NIAGARA.

ERE beings with soul and mind arrayed
Their earthly habitation had made —
When the Saurian monsters in agony lay,
Stricken by doom, on their beds of clay —
Like a meteor, illuming some desolate land,
Niagara leaped from its Maker's hand !

Once spirits of beauty that manhood enslave
At nightfall were seen on its emerald wave ;
In seraphic strain they whispered a song
Whose rapturous concords to Eden belong.
They hunted the thicket with spear and with bow,
Or called the Naiades from their caverns below,
To search for the living trophies that sink
In the green gulf of water that flows o'er the brink

A fairy isle trembles on the cataract's crest,
Beloved by the waves, that hold it compressed ;

And, like worshipping Magii, rainbows arise,
'Neath these acres of paradise dropped from the skies.
Transition and death now dwell in the smile
Of the white, foaming rapids that sweep past the isle ;
Could their waters but cleanse the deep stain of man's sin,
How many a diver the torrent would win !

In vain the Ice-king, whose touch is death,
Would stem the wild current, with Arctic breath ;
With slow-creeping gait, and palsying shock,
Though he bind the cataract fast to the rock,
Long ere the green blade has pierced the ground,
Sunbeams dispel the enchantment around,
And the waters rush on to the far distant sea,
As if wandering their way to eternity.

TELESCOPE AND FIRMAMENT.

STARS of evening, isles of promise,
Hieroglyphics of the skies—
Vainly the Egyptian shepherds
Read your signs, with weary eyes.

Happy we, whose quickened senses
Reach beyond the airy seas,
Where, in space, our life-boat launches—
Hopeful as the " Genoese."

" Colon "* found lost " Atalantis,"
And recovered Earth's domain :
Through the glass we've found our future—
View the homes our spirits gain.

* Christopher Colon, the discoverer of America.

Hail to science! from whose teaching
Rays of revelation beam:
Stars to worlds become exalted
From the beacon-lights they seem.

Thus, the globe shrinks in dimension,
We but fill an atom's place;
Holier climes are floating round us,
Peopled by a mightier race.

When the compact has expired
'Twixt our soul and earthly frame,
And this spirit from its thraldom
Rises like a heavenly flame;

Planet sires our forms may fashion—
Call us from the "vasty deep;"
Out of laps of saintly mothers
We to infant life may creep.

God of wonders! where thy marvels
Stun our mind and stay our breath,
There I read: we shall not perish
In the idleness of death.

LENORE.

TRANSLATED FROM THE GERMAN.

Von Arnim and Brentano, the compilers of a valuable collection of ancient German poems, entitled "Des Knaben Wunderhorn," assert that Burger's ballad "Lenore," is founded on the following poem. Burger, who is guilty of having passed several transla- tions from English authors as his own original compositions, says: he derived the conception of his best achievement from an imperfect refrain that he casually overheard, when sung by a peasant girl. Voss, a good literary scholar, and co-temporary of Burger, remarks that the version incorporated in the collection of Von Arnim and Brentano is equally modern with that of Burger.

ABOVE the stars are twinkling —
The moon is shining bright —
And the dead they ride by night.

"My love, wilt ope thy window;
I cannot long remain,
And may not come again.

"The cock already crows —
Tells of the dawning day,
And warns me far away.

" My journey distant lies ;
Afar with thee, my bride
A hundred leagues we'll ride.

" In Hungary's fair land
I've found a tranquil spot:
A little garden plot.

" And there, within the green,
A little cottage rests,
Befitting bridal guests."

" Oh thou hast lingered long ;
Beloved, welcome here—
Lead on, I'll never fear."

" So, wrap my mantle round ;
The moon will be our guide,
And quick by night we'll ride."

" When will our journey end ?
For heavy grows my sight,
And lonely is the night."

" You gate leads to our home ;
Our bridal tour is done —
My purpose now is won.

" Dismount we from our steed ;
Here lay thy aching head—
This tomb's our bridal bed.

" Now art thou truly mine :
I rode away thy breath—
Thou art the bride of death !"

MARRIAGE.

LOVE'S magnet-like — by instinct hearts are mated;
To live in pairs, we were in pairs created.

   'Tis wedlock wins the heritage of earth;
Then squander not thy claim to man's estate.
Though anchorite and nun lead barren lives,
Ours is the fate to dwell in living hives;
And when at length in death these shores we flee,
Children renew life's bond eternally.

   All ties of home are transient: younger claims
Soon ask a sister's, or a brother's care;
Death leads away our parents, friends enstrange —
Their habits, our convictions, — how they change!
When time has flung its burden on thy back,
What bliss to have a loved-one by thy side,
Who, hand-in-hand, has wandered far with thee.
Toward the portals of eternity.

Seek not 'mong vain and night-parading things
For company with whom to link thy fate :
For them thy purse must golden grains distil,
That they may moult gay feathers at their will ;
To perch in gilded cage on rose-wood frames,
And feed from crystal cups, are all their aims.
By night may'st thou thy paragon dove display—
Although she prove an owl concealed by day—
That wives may envy and men emulate
Home misery and happiness of state !

Go, find some truer type of woman-kind ;
One moved by kindred soul, thy peer in mind,
Whose aspirations will not fail to show
A wife in feeling, a mother in embryo ;
Whose every purpose twining with thine own
Completes itself when both to one are grown.

THE GRENADIERS.

TRANSLATED FROM THE GERMAN OF HEINE.

Most of Heine's Poems have been successfully interpreted by recent
English and American translations.

T'WARDS France were wandering two grenadiers,
  From Russian captivity returning;
And when to the German encampment they came,
  With pain their wounds were burning.

They bowed their heads, when they heard the tale
  That the empire's star had vanished;
Scattered and slain were the heroes of old,
  And Napoleon, the conqueror, banished!

Then together wept these guardsmen old,
  At the tales so oft repeated;
Said one: "Comrade, I sink with shame,
  When I think of our armies defeated."

The other replied: " We are undone !
　　Death soon would hide my anguish,
Had I not wife and child at home,
　　Where now in want they languish."

" I heed not wife, I heed not child,
　　Since our country's greatness has vanished ;
Weep hungry wife, beg orphan child—
　　Our emperor's degraded and banished !

" Comrade, grant me one only boon :
　　If in stranger's land I perish,
Convey my corpse to its native soil—
　　France—the home that we cherish.

" This cross of honor, with ribbon red,
　　To victory shall guide me ;
This musket place in my left hand,
　　And gird my sword beside me.

" Hid in the grave, I'll listen still,
　　Like a picket, lonely camping,
Till I hear the drum's and musket's din,
　　And the cavalry's loud tramping.

" When the emperor returns, to win again
   Lost battle-fields so gory,
Then quick I'll rise, a warrior armed,
   To fight for *'France and glory!'* "

A NIGHT VISION.

I KNOW not how it happened that
One evening, lone and late,
I rested from a weary walk,
Beside a church-yard gate;
The street was hushed, the stars shone out,
The city's lights grew pale;
I heard nought but the watchman's tap,
And night-bird's lonely wail.

I thought of life, its hope and strife,
Of idols 'neath the dust;
And many a deep-set hinge was moved,
That long had gone to rust:
Relentless doom, that youth and strength
Should waste away and fall;
Ah, why is nature's life-crop sown
That death may harvest all!

Thus as I mused a vision crept
From bush and mossy stone :
Methought a muffled form approached,
Like one whom I had known.
The image lived, the image spoke,
In accents soft and slow :
" I bring thee echoes of the grave,
From wanderings below.

" Too early severed were the ties
That clustered 'round my birth ;
Friend-less and child-less have I lived,
Nor e'er knew woman's worth.
The demon of gain soon conquered me,
And I became his slave ;
My purse was haunted with tear and curse,
For I took, but never gave.

" Beneath the sod I sought repose ;
But at the door of death
No welcome came : this worn-out trunk
Refilled with living breath,
And veiled in gloom, a seraph spoke
In tones of wonderous sound :
' Return to life, within this tomb,
No refuge can be found.

" ' The widow and the orphan seek,
   Go, heal their suffering deep,
And o'er life's path sow fertile seed,
   That blessings thou may'st reap.
Through manhood back to infancy
   Thy life once more retrace,
'Till thou at last, a sinless babe,
   Canst meet thy Maker's face.

" ' Electric flashes then illumed
   These eyes so heaven-blind ;
These icy limbs were thawed to life,
   Aroused this feeble mind.
Oh, wearied sense, blunted desire,
   That I from rest am driven,
To spin once more the thread of life,
   And wend my way from heaven !' "

The cricket chirped—the vision fled !
   'Twas dewy morning hour ;
I felt alike some hapless wretch,
   Released from demon-power.
Why did this coward flesh with fear
   Wax motionless, and cold ?
For in a dreaming was to me
   This spectral legend told.

A WINTER'S RIDE.

FOUNDED ON A GERMAN BALLAD BY G. SCHWAB.

I

ON snow-fields shimmers the sunlight clear,
A horseman rides through the forest drear.

Onward he spurs t'ward Constance Lake;
His steed flies, panting, o'er field and brake

Away it strides, to its utmost reach,
Afar in the sky the snow-geese screech;

And the water-fowl flutter, with startled cry,
As the twain, like spectres, are hurrying by.

They would reach the ferry ere night sets in,
In safety the furthermost shore to win.

Not guide nor wayfarer meet their gaze,
To lead them safely o'er trackless ways.

II.

Evening creeps into dusky night;
In the distance glimmers a flickering light.

The ground now rustles with stone and thorn;
Faintly resounds the mountaineer's horn.

Dogs bark loud at the rider's side;
The village-inn opens its portals wide.

" Fair dame at the doorway, that beckonest to me,
How far am I distant from Constance Sea?"

The landlady, lost in wonder, replies:
" Its deep blue water behind thee lies."

The stranger shuddered, and faintly spake:
" I found no ferry—I saw no lake."

Then the startled villager raised her hand:
" 'Twas the ice that bridged thee from land to land!"

And the gathering crowd was heard to say:
"In the keeping of God did he find his way."

III.

" Dismount and partake of cheer and repose;
Warm thy chilled blood that sluggishly flows.

" Recount by the hearthstone thy marvellous ride;
How the sure-footed steed bounded over the tide "

The traveller heard not their welcoming calls:
Faint and benumbed from his horse he falls.

The fearful illusion had stricken his brain
That he rode the snow-fields over again.

He heard the crash, and he felt the wave:
In the abyss of waters he found his grave.

IMMORTALITY.

AFAR we stretch our bold, unbounded thought—
Yearn for a future that we all expect;
Are we a toy, for saintly pastime formed—
Or are we shadows of an angel sect?

Why should our Maker plant a vain desire
Or hopeless aim in our confiding breast?
Why cast us off, like self-deluded clowns,
To waste or perish in our tomb of rest?

Clear-visioned grows the blinded owl by night;
The insect scents its mate, though far away;
The lizard's nerves foretell the coming storm:
We feel the advent of some future day.

Earth's driven sands count many as of yore;
Each cloud, dispersed, in raindrops shall unite;
Thus our stray lives will gather once again
Within their native realm of truth and light.

We know God in his mystery has ordained
That human spirits shall descend to earth,
And that our buried dust may rise again,
To shape some infant struggling for its birth.

But ne'er this mind, that earthly things controls
May linger here, nor shall "to dust return;"
Death—strikes the fetters from our heaven-born souls,
And gleans—our ashes in the mourner's urn.

THE GIANT'S PLAYTHING.

TRANSLATED FROM THE GERMAN OF CHAMISSO.

In Alsace lies a castle, by many a tale renowned,
Within whose walls, in olden time, a giant race was found.
Its towers are decked with mosses and tumbled in decay;
In vain you ask of giants — their race has passed away.

Once went the giant's daughter beyond the fastness strong,
And wandered heedless onward, the rocks and wilds among;
'Neath precipices creeping, she sought the plains below —
Through clouds and mist descending, where glistening
    rivers flow.

With eager step she strided through orchard and o'er field,
T'ward Haslach's blooming valleys, that golden harvests
    yield ;
From forge and mill and cottage, whence smoky vapors
    curled,
She heard the busied humming within the pigmy world.

And as she gazed intently, with wonder-stricken eye,
A lonely peasant wandered within a field of rye ;
Strange seemed the little creature, thus creeping in the
    green,
And like a gem the little plow gleamed with its silvery
    sheen.

" Oh what a pretty plaything within the grass I've found,"
Said she, and quickly spreading her 'kerchief on the ground,
Within its folds of linen the living heap she brushed,
And tied it up with caution, that nothing should be crushed.

Then like a child she gambolled towards the castle's height,
With wond'rous trophies freighted, to glad her parent's sight :
" Come hither, dearest father, strange beings have I found ;
These curious little creatures were crawling on the ground !"

The father sat at table, regaling him with wine—
For giants oft were thirsty, and giants too must dine ;
" What floundering object bringst thou within thy 'kerchief
    tied—
Thou't breathless as a vampire, and giddy as a bride !"

The living heap was lifted and oped with eager hand :
Lo, peasant, plow and oxen before the father stand ;
More curious than playthings that are a child's delight,
So dwarf-like, so amusing they seemed to giant's sight.

Then frowned the earnest parent, and shook his bushy head;
" Restrain thy truant rambles," the stalwart father said ;
" Replace these pilfered tokens, else sorrow comes of joy —
These cattle are not playthings, the peasant is no toy !

" For farmer, plow and oxen purvey our daily food ;
Without their menial labor earth were a solitude ;
Their toil supplies our coffers, and grows our flesh and bone :
We have by others' efforts to size and power grown ! "

In Alsace lies the castle, by many a tale renowned,
Within whose walls, in olden time, a giant race was found ;
Its towers are decked with mosses, and tumbled in decay :
Would that the thoughtful giants had never passed away !

BURIED ALIVE.

In quest of living ruins have I come—
To view the past in this Mausoleum,
Where banished greatness, lost to happier days,
Like moonlight ruins opens to our gaze.

Here dwells the sage who oft, a suitor bold,
Unveiled coy nature—one who could unfold
The springs of human heart—now grown akin
To Nebuchadnezzar, whom the curse of God
Sent to the fields, to pasture on the sod.
Not wit nor learning light that darkened mind;
A seeming Centaur—man and beast combined—
A savage, clown and seer I view in thee—
An ogre come to flesh reality—
Who in this lonely place exhorting calls
Rats from their holes, and spiders from their walls!

Tearful appeals—alas, thou heedst them not!
Long have thy kindred been by thee forgot.
What though thy fame's in every household known,
Thyself to mankind art a stranger grown;
What though thy wasted form partake of bread—
Thy mindless body represents the dead!

Give utterance! That stare which frightful seems,
Can it be "rambling in the land of dreams?"
Teach us to comprehend the signs that tell
Whither with airy shadows thou dost dwell.
Methinks some Eurydice has led astray
To hold thy spirit spell-bound far away?
Hast thou too ardent wooed the Muse of Song—
Too deeply worshipped Bacchus, and too long?
Would that our prayers, with telegraphic speed,
Could reach thy captive spirit in its need;
In vain we call "return thou errant son,
To us, from purgatorial wandering won."

EGYPT.

Where wind-moved sands roll o'er the desert ground,
No flower blooms, nor song-bird flits around;
There, by the moon, the fierce hyena howls
'Mong ruins, where the 'vengeful Bedouin prowls,
Guerrilla-like to slay each Frankish man,
Or overcome th' unguarded caravan.

Monsters forgot are buried 'neath the plain,
And ruined temples lay like giants slain;
There the shame-visaged Sphynx* sinks in her bed,
Whilst the proud pyramid still lifts its head,
Upbraiding time, conversing with the skies—
The desert blast and thunderbolt defies!
The sorcerer's art and wily power unknown
That won these trophies from a distant zone;
Old as geology itself they seem,
Though faint their history, like an infant's dream!

* The profile of this ancient deity was grossly mutilated by the Saracens, during the middle ages. Modern investigation has shown that its colossal body lies deeply sunken beneath the drifted sands of the desert.

The race that planted Thebes above the ground,
That waked these altars to prophetic sound,
Were neither winged nor giant, black nor red.
These catacombs disclose the honored dead,
Whose mummied forms do yet await the day
When souls shall come unto their former clay.
From out these temples came the living word
Of science, and the knowledge of the Lord,
Whence Plato copied, well-taught Moses drew
The inspirations and the truths they knew.
Oh, recent Joseph, shepherd Pharaoh*
None of these ancient Thebans did ye know;
Greek Cleopatras and Ptolemys,
To you were veiled Rameses' mysteries!
On stony page, by chisel skill defined
Time's record lives : our mental vision's blind—
Our cunning's baffled—and the link that bound
Us to the primeval past may ne'er be found.

---

* Historians explain that the term "pharaoh" was a general one, applied to successive rulers of lower Egypt by an alien nomadic tribe, who in the time of "Joseph" had overrun and conquered a portion of the Egyptian territory.

THE RECOGNITION.

TRANSLATED FROM THE GERMAN OF VOGL.

THERE comes a wanderer, staff in hand,
Homeward returning from distant land.

His beard is tangled, his face is brown;
Will they know him again in his native town?

Enraptured he nears the city-gate,
Where the toller of yore is standing in wait.

'Twas a youthful comrade, true and fast;
Once many a wine-cup between them passed.

Yet strange—the toll-gatherer knows him not:
Do beard and sunshine his features blot?

He shakes the dust from his trodden boot;
He turns in silence, with brief salute.

Behold—his true-love stands at the door:
" Thou blooming fair-one, welcome once more!"

But the maid, unconscious, remains unmoved!
She knows not the voice of her once-beloved.

He bends his step t'wards childhood's home;
To his cheek so brown the teardrops come.

Near the cot his mother is wending her way:
" God bless thee, beloved!"—'tis all he can say.

The mother—she turns and shouts with joy;
In her arms she is clasping her truant boy.

Though the sun may swart, and the beard may grow,
The mother, the mother her son doth know.

THE AGE OF PROGRESS.

How happy in this solitude to dwell!
Where whispering thoughts their admonitions tell;
God's handiworks extort my feeble praise;
Each rising sun shall bring me Sabbath days.

Delay ye nights that frost the forests red,
Paint not the leafy shrouds of autumn's dead,
But spare these blooming woodland scenes to me,
Where thought and legend dwell in every tree.

Faint grow the stories of the pioneer;
The revolution's landmarks disappear;
The rustic plow o'erturns th' historic ground,
And ripening grain waves o'er its gore-drenched bound

The yoked kine, the ever plodding mill,
Show nature humbled by man's restless will;
The clover mead and flowered garden-path,
They are the captive valley's epitaph.

Hushed are the war-whoop and respondent scream;
No more the stag, wolf-hunted, seeks the stream;
The stilted crane no longer flaps his wings
On reedy marge, where meek the robin sings.

Where Mohawk hunter chased the woodland herd,
Aloft, like castled knight, the royal bird
Maintains his sway, and views with glaring eyes
The shepherd flock—the marksman's skill defies!

And truant cascades leap from sylvan fount,
Past winding paths, that hug the stalwart mount,
Climbing to heights, from whence, in outlines gray,
Deep shadows consecrate the parting day.

Ye oaks that stand athwart the mountain breeze,
Your tops shall wave in distant India's seas,
And quick as ye receive the woodman's shock,
The powder-fiend shall cleave the stubborn rock!

Anon the granite block shall face the skies,
Reared far on high, where saintly spires arise ;
Lakes shall be drained, mountains by inches fall :
Man's art will smite and overcome them all!

Alas ! beneath this ever-changing moon
The Age of Progress hurries on too soon :
Youth's rosy haunts man's searches ne'er may find—
For fleeting time leaves memory far behind.

EXTERNAL PIETY.

'TIS Sabbath-piety moves the worldly-wise—
'Tis church-religion blinds our credulous eyes;
For refugees an anchor in despair—
A cloak for madness, that fanatics wear.
Though howling wolves would not destroy each other,
Sect curses sect, brother, alas, dooms brother!
Rank orthodoxy is the set-up price
That wins the golden keys of paradise;
Whilst law is studied as the week-day code,
To guide the pious on their worldly road.

Mayhap some eulogy proclaims aloud
A genteel exit from a genteel crowd,
Of one who knelt at prayer with yielding mind,
Thoughtless in zeal, though studiously blind;
Who took the Word entire—a strict believer—
Though God had marked him out an arrant thiever;
Who oft in holy walks forsook his race,
That he might church-ward turn his saintly face.

Chant anthems, and give benedictions! he
Through legacies has bridged eternity.
'Mong chosen men he consecrated lies
Where willows droop and epitaphs arise;
A sickening, solemn mockery of truth,
Doubted by age, but oh! believed by youth.

THE SLEEP OF BARBAROSSA.

TRANSLATED FROM THE GERMAN OF RÜCKERT.

An Olden Legend. Geibel and others have treated the same subject in metre.

THE Emperor Barbarossa
  Still hides in caverns deep,
Among his ancient courtiers,
  Fast bound in magic sleep.

The glory of his empire
  Long since has passed away :
He will revive its splendor,
  At no far-distant day.

Upon a throne of ivory
  Reclines the hero old ;
His mighty arms uplifted
  Both sword and sceptre hold.

The beard that marks the Kaiser
In rays of fire glows,
And through the marble tablet
Into his lap it grows.

He nods, like one inspired,
    And blinks from dreamy eyes;
He draws a breath profoundly—
    Then bids a page arise.

Thus in his trance he speaketh:
" Go boy without, and look
If round this castle-turret
    Still flies the olden rook.

" And if the rook and raven
    Yet dwell beneath these skies,
A hundred years must follow
    Ere from my sleep I'll rise."

THE EXPLORER.

FOREVER onward! rest forbodes decay;
I breathe to live, I live for earthly sway!
My spirit longs, my every sense devours
The scenes that glide away with time's swift hours.

Forever onward! why should distance hide
The land, the ocean—both expanding wide
Toward the polar waste and torrid zone,
Where flame the skies, or verdure is unknown.

I tramp the main, and I invade the sea;
A ruler's stride o'er earth was given me.
Thy term brief, hurried life I dedicate
To search the records of man's huge estate.

When youth no more in living embers glows,
When staff, or crutch, at length ordain repose,
Then may I tell of nobler trophies won
Than thou hast gathered, vain Napoleon.

FADING AWAY.

TRANSLATED FROM THE GERMAN OF STORM.

THE cottage chamber is close and still;
Within is a patient, weak and ill.

His fevered brow throbbed wildly by night;
His heart is sick, his eye shuns light.

He holds the watch in his withered hand,
Whilst his life runs out, like the hour-glass' sand.

In silence he marvels if breath will last
'Till the minute hand thrice o'er the dial has passed.

A faithful attendant is watchful and near,
Awaiting day dawn with sorrow and fear.

Now it dawns! the shadows of midnight depart—
Death slowly winds round that faint throbbing heart.

Up on the window the morning rays creep;
Bird and maiden awaken from sleep.

Freshened nature lives over her youthful hours,
And May-bells ring in the feast of flowers.

Merry young plowmen rove o'er the green,
Where robins are heard, and bright flowers are seen.

Forsaken and lone seems that little room
Where the nurse has watched o'er the sick one's doom.

From his staring eye beams no living light;
His hands are folded stiff and tight.

She has drawn the sheet; without tear or word
She departs; no breathing, no whisper are heard.

WINTER WEATHER.

The quickening flood-rays of sunlight and heat
Stream far away South to the song-bird's retreat.

In feathery flocks frail creatures of air
Alight on the grainfields stiff-frozen and bare.

Like a freebooter prisoned, in penance and woe,
In the belfrey sits hungry the black-a-moor crow.

Bristled pines revel in snowy delight,
As if robed and begemmed for a festival night.

O'er the diamond-decked cot of the emerald vale
The moon sheds its frost-beams spectral and pale.

The blast laps the hearth-fire, and pipes by the door,
Looks in at the window, and searches the floor.

Withered leaves rustle in skeleton groves;
In the rattling tree-boughs the North-Wind roves.

The North-Wind—that tracks the explorer's lost way,
By the chrystalline bridges that span Baffin's Bay:

He has whirled on Earth's axis, and swept the blear pole;
At his coming the surf-bells their monody toll.

THE RECKONER.

TRANSLATED FROM THE GERMAN OF VOGL.

A PLODDING reckoner, with thought intent,
Mindful of gains, o'er his cyphers bent.

Ever his hand the inkstand sought;
He solved in figures the knottiest thought.

Thus toiling and reckoning day by day,
Already his hair was changing to gray.

And silently whispered the man-of-bone:
" Thy balance-sheet, brother, must soon be shown."

Then went the reckoner to view the fields,
And feast on the bounties that nature yields.

Flowers were blooming, fragrant and bright:
But the cyphers, confusing, dimmed his sight.

Birds were piping their careless trill:
But loudly echoed the scratching quill.

Clouds were decked with golden rays:
He saw only visions of inky ways.

'Twas then he cast a penitent look
At desk, and counter, and manuscript book.

Oh mournful the day when he penned each page,
And reckoned glad youth into desolate age!

STARS AND STRIPES.

WE'RE a people — we're a power ---
Nations, heed the solemn word!
Taunt not, lest this revelation
From the cannon's mouth be heard!

Each trained man swings scythe and sabre,
Each boy learns to fight and farm;
Steel and powder are our safeguards —
Keen our vision, strong our arm.

Many empires are absorbed
In this vast and fertile land;
Afric's nor Siberia's deserts
Mockingly our bounds expand.

To bleak climes, where, plant forsaken,
Forge and shuttle work the gains,
Onward sails the peace armada,
Bearing harvests from our plains.

Nevermore shall labor languish,
Paralyzed by tyrant might;
For our " Stars" they are unfurled
To dispel want's cloudy night.

Fierce barbarians must not plunder,
Nor may lorded serfs defy;
For our " Stripes" shall flash upon them,
Like the lightning from the sky,

And when traitor foes are gathered
Where the battle's thunder roars,
Let the blue-gemmed badge mount higher
Than the bird of freedom soars :

Spread from mastheads, crowning mountains,
Streaming o'er the tented field,
Victory e'er betides our heroes—
Right and might will never yield !

WAYFARING.

TRANSLATED FROM THE GERMAN OF RÜCKERT.

I KNOCKED in vain at the rich man's door :
A farthing is all he gives to the poor.

Gently I tapped at affection's gate :
Ten others were wooing, I was too late.

Fain would I approach honor's castled abode :
No spurs had I won, no palfrey I rode.

Where industry toiled, a pittance to gain,
I met only rags, starvation and pain.

Through life have I sought the abode of content :
It beckoned, but vanished when nearer I went.

9

One cottage I found—'twas grassy and low;
Thither for refuge at last I may go.

Its portals are open, to welcome each guest;
There many before me in silence sought rest.

PEDANTRY.

FROM rote and maxim liberate the mind,
That every problem thought-solution find;
For living action best can illustrate
The lineaments of every mind-portrait.
  Our schoolboy teachings, meted out by rule,
Class embryo sage too oft with embryo fool;
And many a pampered Solon leaves his class
Read and accomplished, but matured, alas,
On musty precept—learning's hierophant—
To stifle progress, by his weighty cant;
Whilst fruitful thinkers delve within themselves—
And shun the oracles from library shelves.
The God-like attribute, inventive power,
Has dawned on them, in an inspired hour;
They scatter the dry leaves of barren lore,
And pierce each problem to its very core.

PROCRASTINATION.

TRANSLATED FROM THE OLDEN GERMAN.

"MOTHER, dear mother, hungry am I;
Pray give me food, or else I will die."

"Patience, my child, and thou shalt eat:
Early to-morrow we'll sow the wheat."

To-morrow came, and the wheat was sown;
But the child still moaned with piteous tone:

"Mother, dear mother, hungry am I;
(Pray give me food, or else I will die.")

"Patience, my child, thy longing restrain:
To-morrow morning we'll gather the grain."

And when the sheaves all gathered lay,
Faintly the child was heard to say :

" Mother, dear mother, hungry am I ;
(Pray give me food, or else I will die.")

" Patience, my child, and dry thy tears—
    To-morrow we'll thresh the wheaten spears."

And when the threshing had all been done,
The mournful infant anew begun :

" Mother, dear mother, hungry am I ;
(Pray give me food, or else I will die.")

" Soon, my child, approaches the hour :
    To-morrow the miller will grind the flour."

And after the grain had all been ground,
The child continued its wailing sound :

" Mother, dear mother, hungry am I ;
(Pray give me food, or else I will die.")

" The bread is kneaded, my darling one ;
  To-morrow the baking will be begun."

The bread was baked, at dawn of day
But famished and dead the infant lay.

PHASES OF LIFE.

MAN'S life has phases three-fold, and they blend
To vary the monotony of time.
First are pursuits, where every move is strife,
That creature comforts to the household brings,
From trophies conquered in material things.
As wit encounters wit, so man seeks man,
Outreckoning his fellow where he can,
And gracefully, by action most unkind,
O'ercomes the weak and too confiding mind.
Thus godly men, of carnal instinct, play
A most ignoble part from day to day.

At night we homeward rove, to seek repose;
Our advent there the lonely day's event,
Our plodding changed to greeting and embrace;
We mount a brother's, son's and father's place.
Here streamlet, tree and flock are all our own;
We rule a prince, upon a household throne!

Stolen from sleep, or by the wayside dreamt,
Our spirit life springs to vitality.
In lone communion self responds to self;
What mean our thoughtless aims, we often ask—
Is life a boon, or shall it be a task?
But holier moments come, as from within:
When life's gay panorama no more haunts
With vain allurements our capricious taste,
We find no harvest gleaned from wilted flowers,
And ask "whence fled life's evanescent hours?"
When strife is banished, peace awakes a chord
Of prayerful, joyous tribute to the Lord,
That tells, "the grave is but a shaded way
Leading from visions of an unreal world;
Where death, by silent witchery, transforms
Life's dismal night to light-enchanted day."

VENETIAN GONDOLIERS.

TRANSLATED FROM THE GERMAN OF CHAMISSO.

In purple glows the evening,
And gently rises the gale;
Whilst many a gay gondola
Has trimmed its fluttering sail.

" 'Tis joy," quoth a maid to her lover,
" This roving o'er the brine;
Spread out our sail to the breezes,
Let the helmsman's place be mine."

" Thou steerest too rashly, beloved,
Afar in the open sea:
Our skiff is frail and helpless,
And the waves run wild and free."

" Must I distrust our vessel ?
   Why should I doubt to-day ?
   Who ever in thee confiding,
   In evil hour gave way ?"

" Art frantic ?   Turn the rudder—
   Thou bringst us both to woe;
   Already wind and billow
   Have play with our frail canoe."

" Then let the angry waters
   Have with these planks their play;
   The rudder is unfastened—
   Despair now leads the way !

" From virtue hast thou guided—
   To ruin have I led ;
   Quick, make thy peace with heaven,
   Thy final prayer be said !

" Why tremble, base deceiver,
   Beneath this glittering steel ?
   My agony is deeper
   Than all that thou canst feel.

" Too many a maiden, betrayed,
  In silence pines to death;
  My crowning deed be 'vengeance'—
' Love' be my dying breath."

The youth his hands was wringing,
  Of his own guilt beknown;
  She struck the steel in his bosom,
Then sank it into her own.

A wreck was seen at morning,
  Borne landward by the flood :
  There lay the lifeless lovers,
United in their blood.

THE PLEIADES.

'TWAS leap-year night; fleet time had stayed his round;
Mankind were housed, and fast in slumber bound.
As wearily I on my couch reclined,
Strange fancies lit my lonely wandering mind;
Each nerve seemed quickened by mysterious power,
That stole o'er me, in this lone, stilly hour.
Upon the wall, within reflected light,
Methought I viewed the antics of some sprite:
Softly I rose, half conscious, half in awe,
To near the shadowy vision that I saw.
Then as I gazed from window overhead,
From each star hung a bright, electric thread,
Gleaming like unto meteoric light,
Suspending winged, seraphic, floating forms,
That shone in colors more than rainbow-hued;
That sang in concord more than harmony;
Graceful as flowers, elfins by pedigree —

Higher in form than woman's loveliness —
Whose beauty language falters to express.

  Spell-bound and way-led, did I ask myself
What charm had brought adown each truant elf;
Or if my mind, waked from a fever trance,
Had run astray, to some weird phantom-dance.
Closely I listened, and soft strains I heard,
More dulcet-toned than song of warbling bird.
But soon they ceased, and then the weary sound
Of low-born men and earthly things resound;
The visions floated as thin vapors rise—
The reddening day-break drew them t'ward the skies;
When moonlight paled each found a home afar,
And vanished distant as the polar star.
Out of their song these syren strains remain—
I may not sing, but word them o'er again:

      " Seven are we,
        Of stellar degree,
        Relics from olden
        Mythology.
        To the constellations
        On high we fled,
        Ere the Son-of-Man
        Arose from the dead.

10

" In childhood we roved
    In this valley of death,
    Where our spirits, clay-prisoned,
    Drew heavenly breath ;
    Ere time, the destroyer,
    Bid Olymp pass away,
    And gave life the canker
    Of early decay.

" Slain are Dragon,
    Centaur and Faun ;
    Wood-nymphs have perished,
    The Titans are gone.
    Since fact and reason
    Rule temporal things,
    Men are exalted
    To beggarly kings.

" Serpent and songster
    Rest 'neath the same shade ;
    Felon and judge
    Out of brothers are made ;
    One doomed a vagrant,
    One born princely heir—
    Lifted to greatness,
    Or hurled to despair.

        *   *   *   *   *   *   *   *   *

" Seven are we,
  Of stellar degree,
  Relics from olden
  Mythology.
  To the constellations
  On high we fled,
  Ere the Son-of-Man
  Arose from the dead.

" Since the gods, star-banished
  Were lost to power,
  Spirits of beauty
  Lurk in the flower,
  Or nestle beneath
  The humming-bird's wing,
  And their eyes peer out
  From each gem-decked ring.

" Belted Orion
  Now shimmers above :
  Pursuing the sister
  That fled from his love ;
  With the speed of Atlanta,
  Equipped for the chase
  He has sent the fleet comet
  To seek her in space.

" Safe in the clouds
   The rain-storm is pent;
   Boreal winds
   To their caves are sent;
   The moon have we burnished
   To noon-day light;
   For we sister Pleiades
   Have revels to-night.

" Children of dream-land,
   Guests of the night,
   Sirius beckons
   The hour * * *
   Gather * * *
   Spirits of air,
   * * * away
   From this planet of care."

DEAD AUTHORS.

UNNUMBERED volumes look from yonder shelves
With beggar's mien, and crave our charity,
Stale, and unpetted by the scholar's hand,
Voiceless, in mock-solemnity they stand,
Like tombstone records ; and each title-page
Tells of rash men, drowned in oblivion's sea
By the avenging muse of Poetry.

THE WATER SPRITES.

TRANSLATED FROM THE GERMAN OF HEINE.

A BURLESQUE ON "DER WASSERMAN" AND "LORELEY"

'TIS a festive night: the grove is illumed,
And the guests have rallied for pleasure;
Soon a stranger couple join in the dance
That moves in fantastical measure.

Graceful they swing, lightly they trip,
In ways that some mischief betoken:
They smile at each other, they shake their heads—
'Till the charm by a whisper is broken.

Quoth the maiden: "Sir Knight, I see by thy crest,
With its purple and low-bending lily,
That was plucked from the ocean's bed below,
Thou art not of Adam's family.

" Thou art the Merman, come to decoy
    Some credulous villager's daughter ;
    I knew thee at once, by thy fish-bony teeth,
    And thy bitter perfume of sea-water."

Onward they whirl through the maze of the dance,
    In antics each other outvieing ;
    They smile at each other, they shake their heads—
    Quoth the swain, in soft accents replying :

" Fair lady, thy hand is so searchingly cold—
    Whence came the green gloss of thy tresses ?
    'Tis marvellous why, 'neath this summery sky,
    So mouldy the seam of thy dress is !

" Well did I know, as we joined in the waltz,
    Thou wert none of earth's lap-nursed creatures :
    I knew thee, Loreley, by thy motionless eye,
    And the moon-bleached hue of thy features."

The music grows weary, the dance is done—
    They part with formal greeting :
    They know each other by far too well,
    And shun a similar meeting.

MISERY AND REMORSE.

TRANSLATED FROM THE OLDEN GERMAN.

" JOSEPH, dear Joseph, thou hast blighted my fame,
And doomed thy own Annie to woe and to shame.

" Joseph, loved Joseph, wherever I go,
Despair comes before me—thy sin is my woe.

" And the finger of scorn points to yonder lone field,
Where I, among wretches, my body must yield.

" Have mercy, ye judges, and hasten my end;
My words of forgiveness to Joseph I send."

Soon an ensign came riding, his colors he waved :
The verdict is stayed, from disgrace she is saved.

Oh ensign, brave ensign, too late thy relief :
Death's angel, more speedy, has solaced her grief.

ON WINGS OF SONG AND MUSIC.

TRANSLATED FROM THE GERMAN OF HEINE.

ON wings of song and music,
  Beloved, I'd waft thee away,
To the flowering banks of Ganges,
  Forever blooming and gay.

Its floral realm shall receive thee,
  Illumed by the silent moon;
There the lotus flowers are longing
  To greet their companion soon.

There violets nod and flutter,
  Or gaze on the stars above;
And roses, with eloquent fragrance,
  Recount their legends of love.

Within the spice-groves are lurking
  The innocent, cunning gazelles ;
And distant is heard the rushing
  Of the holy tide, as it swells.

Under the palm will we linger,
  Housed from the open skies,
In raptures of love and contentment—
  Dreaming with open eyes.

TO A COQUETTE.

Vows of love—are only whispered,
Holiest words—are from us wrung;
And the heart's most deep affection
Seldom yet has poet sung.

Maid, 'twere well that others knew thee,
And the danger in thine eyes—
That, like the taper's flame alluring,
Burn the dazzled evening-flies.

Thou hast humbled the confiding,
Mocked at many a lover's vows—
'Till thy bosom's "milk of kindness"
Curdled with corruption flows.

And the venom of thy nature,
Jaundice-like, will spread within,
Until, desperate, thy ambition
Leads thee on to greater sin.

Widowed hearts still linger round thee,
Made more solemn than by death ;
Soon thou'lt shudder at thy loneness—
Curse thy fate, with dying breath.

Beauteous image—of destruction,
Blossom of—the Upas tree,
Silken serpent, I've uncoiled thee :
Never strike thy fangs at me.

www.ingramcontent.com/pod-product-compliance
Lightning Source LLC
Chambersburg PA
CBHW020800020726
47495CB00008B/2523